KT-571-600

RAMPAGE OF THE HUNGRY GIANTS

Dinosaur Cove™

DINOSAUR COVE™

RAMPAGE OF THE
HUNGRY GIANTS

by
REX STONE

illustrated by
MIKE SPOOR

Series created by
Working Partners Ltd

OXFORD
UNIVERSITY PRESS

Special thanks to Jane Clarke

To Ros, my fossiliferous friend. R.S.

These illustrations are for Sarah Darby
for her patience and skill. M.S.

OXFORD
UNIVERSITY PRESS

Great Clarendon Street, Oxford OX2 6DP
Oxford University Press is a department of the University of Oxford.
It furthers the University's objective of excellence in research, scholarship,
and education by publishing worldwide in

Oxford   New York

Auckland Cape Town Dar es Salaam Hong Kong Karachi
Kuala Lumpur Madrid Melbourne Mexico City Nairobi
New Delhi Shanghai Taipei Toronto

With offices in

Argentina Austria Brazil Chile Czech Republic France Greece
Guatemala Hungary Italy Japan Poland Portugal Singapore
South Korea Switzerland Thailand Turkey Ukraine Vietnam

Oxford is a registered trade mark of Oxford University Press
in the UK and in certain other countries

British Library Cataloguing in Publication Data

Data available
ISBN: 978-0-19-272978-1

Printed and bound by Clays Ltd, St Ives plc

Paper used in the production of this book is a natural,
recyclable product made from wood grown in sustainable forests
The manufacturing process conforms to the environmental
regulations of the country of origin

FACT FILE

➡ JAMIE'S DAD'S MUSEUM ON THE BOTTOM FLOOR OF THE LIGHTHOUSE IN DINOSAUR COVE IS THE SECOND BEST PLACE IN THE WORLD TO BE. THE FIRST IS DINO WORLD, OF COURSE, THE SECRET THAT JAMIE AND HIS BEST FRIEND TOM HAVE DISCOVERED IN THE BACK OF A DEEP, DARK CAVE. NOT ALL THE DINOSAURS THAT THE BOYS MEET WANT TO EAT THEM, BUT EVEN PLANT-EATERS CAN BE DANGEROUS.

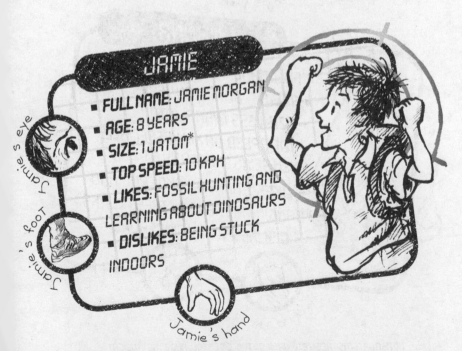

JAMIE

- **FULL NAME:** JAMIE MORGAN
- **AGE:** 8 YEARS
- **SIZE:** 1 JATOM*
- **TOP SPEED:** 10 KPH
- **LIKES:** FOSSIL HUNTING AND LEARNING ABOUT DINOSAURS
- **DISLIKES:** BEING STUCK INDOORS

Jamie's eye

Jamie's foot

Jamie's hand

*NOTE: A JATOM IS THE SIZE OF JAMIE OR TOM: 125 CM TALL AND 27 KG IN WEIGHT

TOM

- **FULL NAME:** THOMAS CLAY
- **AGE:** 8 YEARS
- **SIZE:** 1 JATOM*
- **TOP SPEED:** 10 KPH
- **LIKES:** TRACKING ANIMALS AND EXPLORING WILDLIFE
- **DISLIKES:** RAINY DAYS

Tom's eye

Tom's hand

WANNA

- **FULL NAME:** WANNANOSAURUS
- **AGE:** 65 - 80 MILLION YEARS**
- **SIZE:** LESS THAN A JATOM*
- **TOP SPEED:** 50 KPH, ESPECIALLY WHEN BEING CHASED BY A T-REX
- **LIKES:** STINKY GINGKO FRUIT AND BANGING HIS HEAD ON TREE TRUNKS
- **DISLIKES:** SCARY DINOSAURS

Wanna's head

Wanna's foot

*NOTE: A JATOM IS THE SIZE OF JAMIE OR TOM: 125 CM TALL AND 27 KG IN WEIGHT
**NOTE: SCIENTISTS CALL THIS PERIOD THE LATE CRETACEOUS

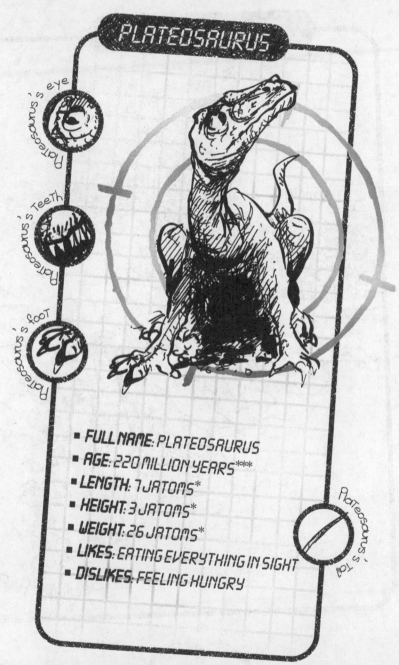

PLATEOSAURUS

Plateosaurus's eye

Plateosaurus's teeth

Plateosaurus's foot

Plateosaurus's tail

- **FULL NAME:** PLATEOSAURUS
- **AGE:** 220 MILLION YEARS***
- **LENGTH:** 7 JATOMS*
- **HEIGHT:** 3 JATOMS*
- **WEIGHT:** 26 JATOMS*
- **LIKES:** EATING EVERYTHING IN SIGHT
- **DISLIKES:** FEELING HUNGRY

*NOTE: A JATOM IS THE SIZE OF JAMIE OR TOM: 125 CM TALL AND 27 KG IN WEIGHT
***NOTE: SCIENTISTS CALL THIS PERIOD THE TRIASSIC

DINOSAUR COVE

Village

Marina

Sealight Head

Landslips where
clay and fossils are

DINO CAVE

High Tide beach line

— Low Tide beach line

Sea

Smuggler's Point

9

'Something's creeping up on us,' Jamie Morgan whispered to his best friend Tom Clay, as they crawled commando-style through the undergrowth in the woods high above the beach.

'Then let's hide here,' Tom hissed, flattening himself to the ground. His freckly, charcoal-streaked face peeked out from behind a bush as he scanned the woods behind them.

Jamie crouched down and held his breath

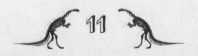

as a big round object covered with sticks and
leaves parted the dried ferns.

'Ahoy, there!' a cheery voice called.

'Grandad.' Jamie laughed. 'You found us in
mega-quick time.'

'Well, look behind you.' Grandad's old
mesh-covered camouflage helmet wobbled as
he grinned. 'You left an obvious trail.'

Jamie and Tom glanced back the way they
had come. Two lines of bare earth led up to
their hiding place.

Grandad picked up a dead branch and
used it to brush leaves over the ground behind

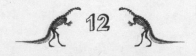

him. 'Basic commando training: cover your tracks if you don't want to be followed. Now, what are your other survival skills like?' he asked.

'Not bad.' Jamie looked at Tom. Grandad had no idea that they'd survived meeting ferocious dinosaurs countless times! Only they knew about the secret cave in Dinosaur Cove that led to Dino World, a land of living, breathing, prehistoric beasts.

'Would you eat this to survive?' Grandad indicated a pink-brown toadstool sprouting from a tree trunk.

'No way,' Tom said. 'Toadstools can be deadly poisonous, even ones that look like mushrooms.'

'Right. But what about this?' Grandad pointed to a fat beetle grub wriggling through the leaf mould. 'Can you eat it?'

'You're joking!' Jamie made a face.

'Lots of grubs are edible.' Grandad picked up the wriggly grub. 'Want a nourishing snack? Chewy on the outside and soft and creamy in the middle . . .'

'Gross!' Jamie pulled a face. He took off his backpack and rummaged through it. His precious Fossil Finder, his notebook with the Triassic map, and the Triassic fossil ammonite were still there from their last trip to Dino World, plus extra survival supplies. He took out an energy bar and handed a piece to Grandad and Tom. 'Much tastier than grubs,' he mumbled with his mouth full.

'Well,' Grandad said, putting down the squirming grub. 'I'll leave you to carry on with your survival training. See you at the lighthouse before dinner.'

Jamie and Tom grinned at each other. They knew just the right place to put what they'd learned into practice . . .

They raced through the woods to the cliff edge, and scurried down the path to the cave on Smuggler's Point. They squeezed through the gap in the back of the cave into the secret chamber. Jamie could feel excitement tingling up from his toes as he stepped into the five fossil dinosaur footprints that led across the floor of the cave.

In an instant, with a blinding flash of light, he was standing inside the hollow tree in Triassic Dino World. And a moment later Tom was beside him. A dragonfly the size of a paper aeroplane whirred past and pine needles crackled beneath their feet as they stepped out into the hot dry Triassic forest.

'Race you to that tree commando-style!' Tom said, dropping to the ground.

Jamie threw himself onto the pine-needly floor of the Triassic forest. A creamy grub the size of a fat sausage wriggled across his path.

'Want a nourishing snack?' he asked Tom.

'Shhh, fossil brain!' Tom hissed. He pointed ahead with a shaking finger. 'That

fern's moving. Something's hiding in it,
waiting to pounce on us when we pass.'

A scaly two-legged dinosaur leapt out of
the bush and hurled itself on them.

'Ambush!' Jamie yelled.

The dinosaur sat on Jamie's chest and licked his face with its long sandpapery tongue.

Sluuurp!

It was Wanna, their dinosaur friend, who accompanied them on all their adventures.

'Geddoff, Wanna!' Jamie spluttered, struggling to his feet.

The little wannanosaurus scampered over to Tom, wagging his tail.

'He was lying in wait for us,' Tom laughed, patting Wanna on his bony skull. 'He'd make

a good commando!'

Grunk, grunk, grunk!

Wanna nosed at Jamie's backpack.

'Sorry, Wanna, no stinky gingko fruit today,' Jamie said. 'We'll have to track down another sort of snack for you.'

Grunk!

Wanna froze and put his head to one side.

'He does that when he senses something.' Tom scanned the dense Triassic forest. 'But I can't see anything...'

'Listen!' Jamie cupped his hand round

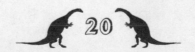

his ear. He could hear something above the insects' buzzing.

Krumph, krumph,

kruuumph!

'It sounds like a giant snoring,' he said. 'A giant dinosaur.'

'Let's check it out,' said Tom.

The noise became louder and more frequent.

'There's more than one,' Tom warned. 'What if they're meat-eaters?'

'They won't see us if we stalk 'em like Grandad showed us,' Jamie said.

They dropped back on their stomachs and began elbowing their way towards the sound. Wanna plopped onto his plump, scaly tummy and followed the boys, propelling himself through the pine needles with his strong back legs. Crawling commando-style in the hot

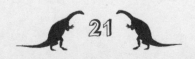

thin Triassic air was much harder than in the
wood in Dinosaur Cove.

'Wanna's not bothering to cover *his* tracks,'
Tom puffed, glancing over his shoulder. 'He's
leaving a trail like a caterpillar tractor!'

'That's OK. Nothing's tracking us; we're
tracking *them*.' Jamie stopped at the edge of
a clearing in the forest, hidden by horsetails.
The clearing was crammed full of long-necked
dinosaurs with small heads and bulky bodies
covered in splotchy red-brown markings like
desert camouflage.

'Plant eaters,' Tom breathed as he, Jamie, and Wanna hunkered down behind a clump of horsetail ferns on the edge of the clearing. 'But what sort?'

'I'll check.' Jamie flipped open the Fossil Finder and, as soon as the Happy Hunting screen popped up, he punched in *TRIASSIC DINOSAUR WITH LONG NECK*. He showed the pictures that popped up to Tom.

'Plateosaurs!' they agreed.

Jamie stowed the Fossil Finder in his backpack, then craned his neck round the horsetails. A few of the platties were on all fours snuffling in a damp patch on the ground. Most were standing on their hind legs, rearing up into the trees. They were krumphing as they jostled each other, stretching out their necks to munch on the pine needles.

'They've got cheek pouches like hamsters,'
Tom said, watching the platties' cheeks
bulging as they chewed.

'Imagine having a pet hamster that's bigger
than an elephant,' Jamie said.

'You'd need a really big cage,' Tom chuckled.

'And lorry loads of hamster food!' Jamie
looked at the chomping dinosaurs. 'These
platties are eating machines.'

Tom pointed to a platty holding on to a branch with a strong hooked claw. 'They've almost got thumbs to help them stuff themselves.'

'Awesome!' Jamie murmured. 'They've stripped the trees almost bare.'

'And it looks like there was a waterhole here, before they drank it all,' Tom added.

Grunk!

Wanna stared at the damp spot in the centre of the clearing. The boys followed his glance. A baby plateosaurus, the size of Wanna, was nuzzling at the barren ground. Then it staggered across to the nearest tree and stood shakily on its hind legs. It stretched out its neck to a small tuft of pine needles but they were well out of its reach.

K-k-krumph!

It cried piteously,
falling back on all fours.

'It's ever so thin,' Jamie
said. 'I can see its ribs...'

The biggest plateosaurus
made a sudden loud

UMPH!

The platties began to
shift around, stamping their feet. Then, one
by one, the herd filed out of the clearing, with
the baby trailing behind.

'Let's track them!' Tom said, dodging from
the horsetails to behind a tree to keep out of
sight.

They followed the great dinosaurs as they
crashed through the undergrowth to the edge
of the forest. A blast of heat hit them as they
looked out across a desert wasteland. Wind-
worn pinnacles of red rock and craggy lava

turrets loomed out of the dusty
sun-scorched earth.

'The platties can't cross that, can they?'
Jamie said as the herd of dinosaurs strode into
the desert, kicking up clouds of dust. 'There's
no food or water out there.'

'I don't think the baby could,' Tom replied.

The baby's head was drooping and its legs
were wobbling as it struggled to keep up.
Jamie could hear it making pathetic uff-uff
noises.

'Its legs are giving way,' Jamie said.

Wanna grunked softly.

Jamie sighed with relief as the leader loped back towards the baby. 'Phew!'

The big platty tried to nudge the baby to its feet, but the baby was too weak to stand. The leader began to sniff at it, but when the baby didn't move, the leader started loping away.

'Oh no!' Tom exclaimed. 'The herd is leaving!'

Jamie gasped. 'But there's no way the baby can survive in the desert on its own. They're leaving it behind to die!'

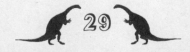

CHAPTER 3

'The leader has to think of the herd,' Tom said as they watched the plateosaurs march away. 'If they stay in the desert with the baby, others might die, too.'

'Then it's up to us to look after it,' Jamie announced.

'It'd be awesome to bring up a baby dino,' Tom agreed. 'But we can't take it home.'

'I know that, fossil brain,' Jamie said. 'We'll help it get better, then get it back to the herd.'

'What? Wander across the desert to find them?' Tom sounded doubtful.

'They're leaving tracks, and they look as if they know where they're going. I'll check the Fossil Finder for clues.' Jamie flipped it open and as soon as the 'Happy Hunting' screen popped up, he typed in PLATEOSAURUS.

'Plateosaurs were great survivors,' he read. 'They ate mostly plants, but scientists think they would gobble up anything small enough to fit into their mouths. They trekked from one place to another in search of food.'

'So the platties know what they're doing, and we can follow their footprints. Come on!' Jamie headed into the dusty desert towards the baby platty, closely followed by Tom and Wanna.

'Hot, hot, hot!' Tom panted, pulling his T-shirt over his head to protect himself from the sun.

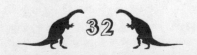

'Wanna likes it,' Jamie coughed as Wanna scampered alongside, kicking up a cloud of red-brown dust.

They weren't far from the baby platty
when five chicken-sized two-legged dinosaurs
with long toothy jaws gathered round the
baby as it lay collapsed on the sand.

Jamie and Tom stopped to quickly consult
the Fossil Finder.

'Procompsognathus,' Jamie said, stashing
the Fossil Finder in his backpack. 'Meat eaters!'

'Like vultures...' Tom said.

The boys looked at each other in dismay.
Then they broke into a run, waving their
arms and yelling.

Gak, gak, gak!

Wanna lowered his bony head and charged.

The little scavenger dinos hissed, showing
their sharp spiky teeth. Then, with a whip of
their scaly tails, they scattered.
The procompys retreated to a safe distance
and re-grouped, watching.

Wanna gently
nosed the baby
dinosaur as Jamie
and Tom knelt
down beside it.

The baby platty
whimpered at
them.

Uff, uff.

'It has to have a drink,' Jamie said, taking out his water flask. But every time he tried to get the flask in the baby's mouth, it turned its head away.

'It's used to lapping water out of a waterhole,' Tom said. 'Maybe it will drink from my hands.' Tom cupped the palms of his hands together to form a drinking bowl and Jamie poured in some water.

Wanna bent over and took a big gulp.

'That's it, Wanna! Show the baby how to do it!' Jamie said.

At the sound of Wanna slurping, the baby platty lifted its head. Tom moved his cupped hands beneath its snout. He beamed as the baby dinosaur swilled up the water. Jamie emptied the rest of his flask into Tom's hands.

'It's still very weak,' Jamie said, when the platty had finished every last drop. 'It must be hungry.' He unwrapped an energy bar and thrust it under the platty's snout.

The baby turned its head away.

Grunk, grunk, grunk!

Wanna ran over to a pile of loose stones and began turning them over with his snout.

'What's he doing?' mumbled Jamie as he stuffed half the energy bar into his mouth and handed the rest to Tom.

'Looking for something . . .' Tom spluttered with his mouth full.

Grunk!

The little wannanosaurus leapt back, wagging his tail, and started to jump about.

Jamie and Tom rushed over to see. Wanna

37

was dancing around a writhing mass of fat sausage-shaped grubs.

'Well done, Wanna,' Tom said. 'The platty might eat one of those.'

Jamie poked one of the grubs. It was soft and squidgy and it wriggled like an enormous worm.

The baby platty paused, sniffing the air.

Uff, uff, uff!

It wobbled to its feet.

The boys and Wanna watched in delight as it staggered over and stuck its snout into the colony of grubs.

Pop! A grub burst between the baby's teeth, then another and another.

'Gross!' Tom and Jamie cringed as the grubs squished and squelched in the baby platty's jaws. Soon creamy grub juice was dribbling down its chin.

Urp!

It burped loudly in Wanna's face.

Gak!

Wanna spluttered as grub slime splattered over his snout.

The baby platty licked the goo off Wanna's nose.

'Grandad was right,' Jamie laughed. 'Grubs *are* a nourishing snack.'

Suddenly, Wanna lowered his head and whipped round.

'The vultures are gathering,' Tom breathed. 'There are nine of them now.'

The procompsognathuses had formed a semi circle and were edging towards them, making pock-pock-pock noises, and scratching the ground with their viciously clawed feet.

pock
pock

pock

'Like killer chickens waiting for a feed,'
Tom whispered.

Jamie glanced towards the other platties.
They were disappearing into the distance.

'We've got to get this baby moving towards
its herd,' Jamie said, 'before the vultures
attack!'

CHAPTER 4

Jamie gingerly picked up a handful of fat wrinkly grubs and held one out to the baby platty.

'Come on!' he said, backing away as the platty stretched out its neck.

The platty took a step towards him, then another and another. It lunged at the grub and hoovered it up. Then it stomped along between the boys, being led along each time Jamie offered him a grub.

'It's getting its strength back!' Tom said.

They plodded through
the sun-baked desert in the dusty
footprints left by the herd of plateosaurs.

Wanna brought up the rear, occasionally
glancing over his shoulder and uttering a
warning grunk at the procompys. As the
platty tracks led uphill, the scavenging dinos
fell back.

The heat haze shimmered all around them
and Jamie pulled out Tom's water flask and
took a swig from it. He handed it to Tom, but
as he was passing it over, it fell. Tom leapt to
catch it, bumping into Jamie as he did so, and

they landed with a
bump right on top of a waist-high
plant covered in prickles.

'Owwww!' Jamie and Tom yelled.

'At least I saved the water flask,' Tom said, as the boys pulled cactus spines out of their clothes. 'We're going to need it in this heat!'

Wanna grunked happily and took a bite from a fat shiny leaf.

The baby platty grabbed at the cactus with its scaly thumbs and began to gobble the leaves whole. The boys watched the juice dribble down the two dinosaurs' chins.

'Cactus contains a lot of water.' Tom carefully broke off a bulbous leaf, grasped it between the spines and squeezed. 'It's not bad,' he said, gingerly licking the juice from the palm of his hand. 'Try some.'

Jamie squeezed some cactus juice into his mouth. It tasted of warm cucumber.

'The baby's gobbling every leaf in sight!' he said, quickly stowing some of the big fat leaves in his backpack. Soon the cactus was stripped bare.

Krumph, krumph, krumph!

The baby looked round for more.

'Platties sure are piggies,' Tom commented.

The platty looked up at him, its jaws caked
with cactus juice. It did a little skip and began
chasing its tail.

'It's feeling a lot better,' Tom grinned.

Grunk!

Wanna gently head-butted the baby platty,
then ran behind a boulder. His tail stuck out
from behind the cone-shaped base.

Umph! Umph!

The baby ran after him.

'They're playing!' Tom laughed as
the platty found Wanna and
butted him back. Then it
ran over and butted
them, too, and ran off
and hid behind a
pile of rocks.

Jamie and Tom
raced after the
baby dino.

'Butt-ya!' Jamie

head-butted the little platty and Tom, and darted behind a pile of blown sand.

'Butt-ya back!' Tom head-butted Jamie in the chest and dashed off.

'Your head's harder than Wanna's,' Jamie gasped as Tom ducked behind a rock.

Jamie, Wanna, and the platty set off after him.

'Butt-ya!' They all head-butted Tom at the same time and landed in a tangled heap on top of him.

'That was fun,' Jamie said. 'The platty's fine now.'

'I'm not!' Tom gasped. He wiped his sweaty brow. 'I need a drink.'

Jamie handed him the flask. Tom took a glug of water and handed it back to Jamie.

'There's only one sip left,' Jamie said, looking worried. 'And I'm really thirsty.'

'You better have it then,' Tom said. 'And hope there is some water by those trees up ahead.'

'I just hope it's not a mirage,' Jamie said, finishing the water. 'Heat plays tricks on your eyes. I've heard of desert explorers thinking they've reached a lake in an oasis, and they dive into it to discover it's just sand.'

'If it is, then we're in big trouble,' Tom said, tipping the empty water flask upside down and peering across the shimmering desert. 'We need water to survive!'

CHAPTER 5

A low krumphing sound echoed across the desert.

'The platties aren't far away,' Jamie said. 'Maybe they will lead us to water?'

Suddenly the heads of the platties came into view behind a sand dune.

The little baby picked up its pace and was soon running through the desert towards the lines of marching platties. The boys and Wanna struggled to keep up.

The baby squealed.

Umph!

The herd of plateosaurs turned as the baby scampered towards them. The adults at the back sniffed at the baby and nosed it gently towards the leader. The boys and Wanna raced round to the front of the herd, just in time to see the big platty gently nuzzle the baby.

'They've accepted it back into the herd,' Tom said with a sigh of relief.

'And there really *are* trees ahead!' Jamie grinned.

'It's an oasis!'

While the

platties plodded along, Jamie, Tom, and
Wanna hurried into a thicket of tall tree palms
and pushed their way through the leaves.

A spring bubbled out of a rocky outcrop
right by where they were standing, filling a
crystal clear blue lake. Across the lake, a group
of waist-high brown lizards with long necks
and tails and blunt snouts stopped drinking
and looked up.

A distance away from the lizards, creatures
the size of big crocodiles, but with beaks like
snapping turtles, hauled

themselves out of the lake to bask in the sun. Wanna stared at the strange creatures, then tiptoed down to the lakeside and began to slurp up the refreshing water.

'This place is awesome,' Jamie whispered, filling up the flasks as quietly as he could so as not to disturb the oasis creatures. The boys had a good long drink, poured some cool water over their heads, and re-filled the flasks for the return journey.

'I need a break before we go back,' Tom said, sitting on a rock in the shade beside the spring.

'Me, too. And I want to find out what these creatures are.' Jamie leant against a shady tree and flipped open the Fossil Finder. Wanna curled up beside him as he studied the information that popped up on the screen. 'Those brown lizards are azendohsaurs and the turto-diles are reptiles called rhynchosaurs,' he told Tom.

Suddenly the tree he was leaning on began to shake. Jamie jumped to his feet as the leader plateosaurus trundled past, followed by the baby, which turned and umphed at him.

Jamie and Wanna hurriedly moved and sat beside Tom as the rest of the herd crashed into the oasis. Everywhere they looked, plateosaurs were muscling in on the water's edge, slurping it up in great mouthfuls, before turning to strip the trees of their leaves.

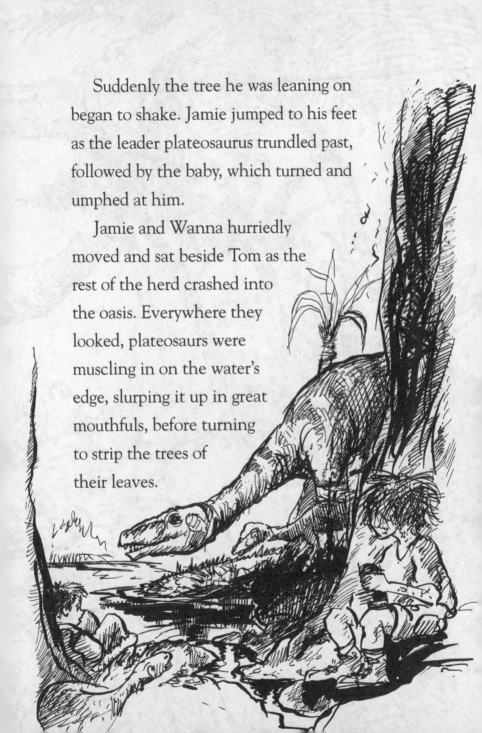

Bleah!

The oasis creatures were not happy about the invasion. The rhinkies snapped at the platties and slipped into the water.

'Uh oh,' Jamie said.

'The platties are eating everything in sight,' Tom said. 'Before long, this oasis will be as bare as the clearing in the forest. Then nothing will be able to survive here.'

'No wonder the rhinkies are mad,' Jamie agreed.

'They don't like us, either,' Tom said. Floating on the water, the rhinkies eyed the boys and Wanna suspiciously.

'Maybe we should get out of here,' Jamie murmured.

'Not before we've moved the herd on,' said Tom. 'We have to save the oasis!'

CHAPTER 6

'But how?' Jamie said. 'We don't have grubs big enough to lure the platties away.'

'And, if we're not careful, we'll end up as rhinky dinner,' Tom replied.

Just then, Wanna raced past the boys, threaded his way through the legs of the adult plateosaurs and head-butted the baby standing at the water's edge.

'This is no time to play, you bonehead!' Tom called, as the baby platty butted Wanna back.

Tom tried to wave Wanna over, but the two small dinosaurs were having too much fun.

The platty did an extra forceful head-butt, sending a happy Wanna tumbling into the trees. To the boys' surprise, Wanna skipped off through the trees, away from the water.

'Come back, Wanna!' Jamie called. Wanna was heading out of the oasis in the wrong direction.

Umph!

The baby ran after its wannanosaurus friend. The leader of the herd lifted its head and bellowed at the baby, but it didn't come back.

'We'd better go after them,' Jamie said. 'We don't want to lose Wanna.'

'Or the baby when
it's just come back to
its herd,' Tom said.

As the boys began
to run, the lead
platty turned. The
rest of the platties
stopped munching
and shuffled their feet.
Then, the leader took
a few steps into the
trees, and the other
platties followed.

'I see!' Jamie said. 'Clever
Wanna! The herd will follow the leader,
so if the leader follows the baby . . .'

'And the baby follows Wanna . . .' Tom
looked at Jamie and grinned. 'We can get
the platties out of the oasis. I was wrong;
this *is* the time to play!'

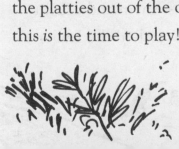

The boys sprinted after Wanna and
the baby. The two dinosaurs were playing
butt-ya in the sand dunes on the other side of
the oasis.

'This way,' they yelled to Wanna, skidding
on the baking hot sand as they raced away
from the trees.

Grunk!

Wanna butted the baby, and the baby
followed.

UMPH!

The leader of the platties bellowed.

Krumph, krumph, krumph!

The rest of the herd took up the call. Jamie
looked over his shoulder.

'It's working; they're leaving the oasis,' he
panted.

Wanna trotted back to the boys as the
herd of dinos trekked past them and caught
up with the baby. They watched the leader

nudge the baby in line and lead the herd up
a steep ridge of sand. At the top, the platties
fanned out along the ridge and stood gazing
into the distance. The baby platty turned and
umphed at them.

'What are they looking at?' Jamie took a
swig of water from his flask and began to slog
up the baking sand, followed by Tom and
Wanna. They hauled themselves up the
steep ridge beside the baby platty.

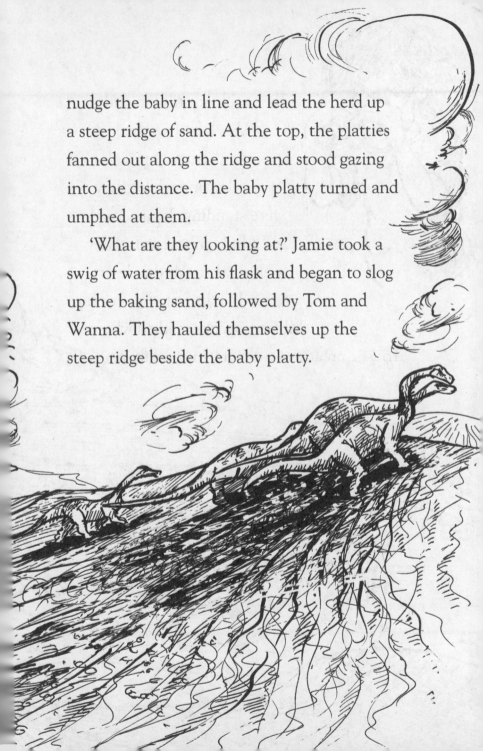

Tom took out his binoculars.
'Wow!' he breathed,
passing them to Jamie.
Far beyond where they
were standing, Jamie could
see a lush green river valley
snaking through the desert
towards a distant white ocean.
Moving specks marked where
Triassic creatures were grazing and flying

through the skies.

'Platty paradise!' Jamie grinned. 'This is where they were headed all along. The oasis was just a pit-stop.'

'I think they've been there before,' Tom said thoughtfully as the leader of the herd lowered its head and swished its tail. 'Like in Africa, where wildebeest have grazing areas they migrate to. They eat all the plants, then they go away and the plants grow again...'

'And they come back . . .' Jamie added.

The plateosaurs were stirring now, shifting from foot to foot.

Grunk!

Wanna touched noses with the baby platty, as if he knew he had to say goodbye.

The boys and Wanna watched as the baby platty and the rest of the herd set off towards the valley.

'Mission accomplished!' Jamie gave Tom a high five. They turned back the way they had come.

The azendohsaurs and rhinkies were snoozing peacefully in the shade as the boys re-filled their flasks at the oasis.

'Time to go back,' Jamie said. 'Before the rhinkies wake up.'

They re-traced the platties' trail through the baking desert, until they reached the crackling needles of the Triassic forest.

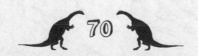

'It's good to be out of the sun,' Tom said, wiping his forehead on his sleeve.

'It's a *bit* cooler in here,' Jamie agreed as they followed their commando tracks back to the hollow tree.

Jamie delved in his backpack.

'We have to go back now, Wanna,' he said, carefully setting the cactus he'd picked from the crater on the ground in front of their little dinosaur friend.

Wanna settled down on the dry pine needles and began to squish up the juicy leaves.

'Bye, Wanna, see you next time,' the boys called, stepping backwards into the dinosaur footprints.

A moment later, the boys were in the secret chamber of the cave in Dinosaur Cove. They raced back to the old lighthouse.

Grandad was just starting to cook dinner. 'Just in time, boys! I collected up a few of those grubs and thought we'd have them for dinner.'

Jamie and Tom looked at each other in panic. 'Really?'

'Sure!' Grandad said and showed them the pot he was stirring. It was filled with globs of white floating in a brown sloshing sauce.

'You'll stay for dinner, won't you, Tom?' Grandad said.

'Um.' Tom wouldn't meet

Grandad's eye. 'I ...
um ... have to ...'
Grandad started
to chuckle.

Jamie decided that
something suspicious was
going on. He grabbed a spoon,
fished out a white globule and
gave it a sniff.

'Is this really a grub?' Jamie
asked Grandad.

'Why don't you try it and find out?'
Grandad replied, with a twinkle in his eye.

'Ew!' Tom said, grimacing.

Jamie took a deep breath, and popped the
spoon in his mouth. A beefy bready flavour
warmed his tongue. 'Mmmm,' Jamie said.
'Delicious!' He grinned at his best friend.
'Are you sure you don't want to stay for
dinner?'

Tom looked from Grandad to Jamie and back again.

Jamie couldn't hold a straight face a moment longer. 'It's beef stew and dumplings.'

'Yummy!' shouted Tom. 'I'm definitely staying!'

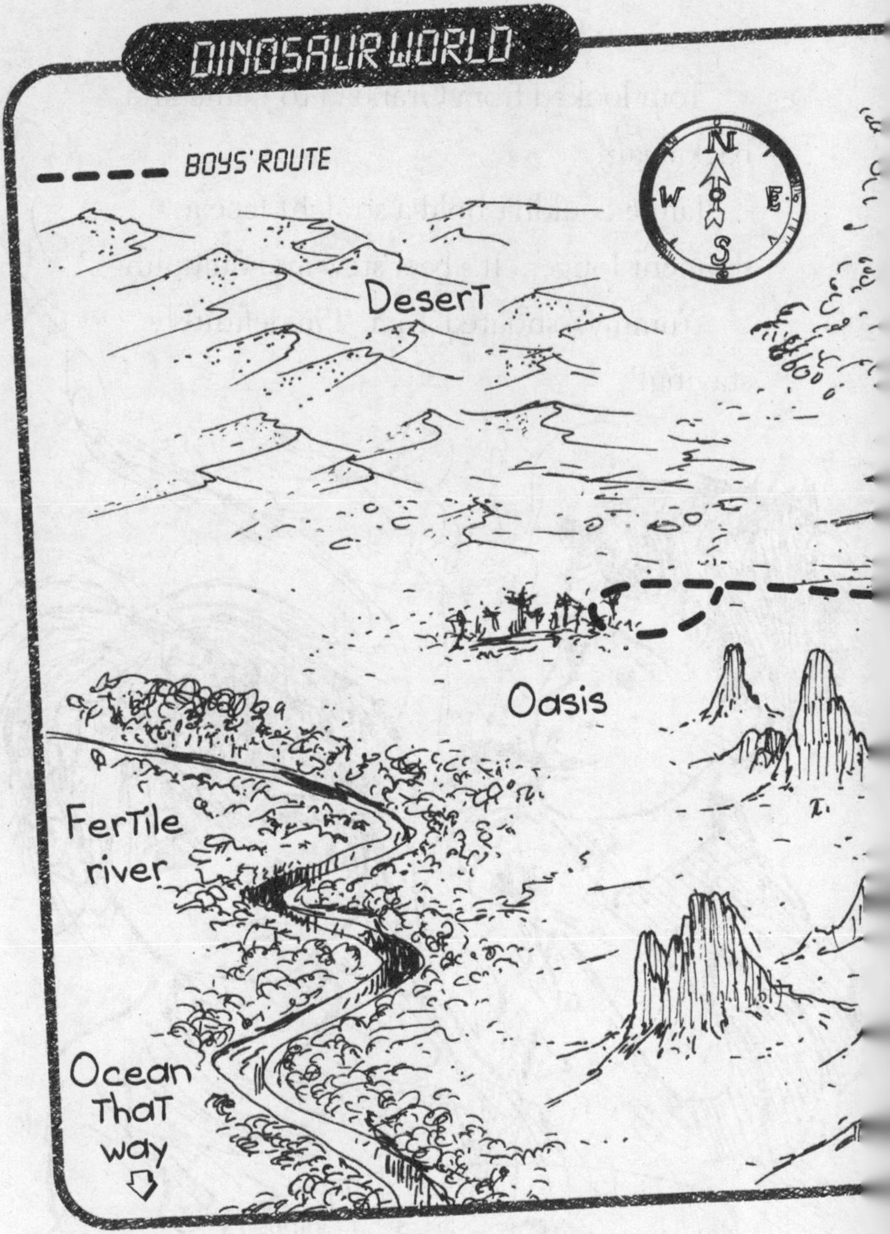
DINOSAUR WORLD
BOYS' ROUTE
N
W
E
S
Desert
Oasis
Fertile river
Ocean That way

Red Mountain

Forest

Dried out river bed

Hollow Tree

Pond

Scrubland

GLOSSARY

Azendohsaurus (az-en-doh-sor-us) – a small dinosaur with a long neck that reached up to waist-height and a long tail. It had a blunt snout, small jaws, and ate plants.

Camouflage (cam-oh-fl-ah-j) – a pattern, like a tiger's stripes, which can help an animal or object blend into the background. Animals and dinosaurs use camouflage to hide from predators.

Gingko (gink-oh) – a tree native to China called a 'living fossil' because fossils of it have been found dating back millions of years, yet they are still around today. Also known as the stink bomb tree because of its smelly apricot-like fruit.

Mirage (mir-ah-j) – an illusion, caused when extreme heat makes the air shimmer and reflect light in unusual ways. This can trick people into thinking that there is an oasis ahead in the desert because the ground appears to sparkle like water.

Oasis (oh-ay-sis) – an area in the desert where there is a spring or other source of water. Plants and trees grow around the water and desert animals often live nearby or regularly travel to the oasis to drink.

Plateosaurus (plat-ee-oh-sor-us) – a large, heavily built dinosaur with a very small head. It could walk on its back legs and had a long neck so it could reach into trees and eat the leaves.

Procompsognathus (pr-oh-komp-sog-nay-thus) – a tiny meat-eating dinosaur with two long back legs and a long snout full of razor-sharp teeth. It ate mainly insects and other small lizards.

Rhynchosaurus (rin-koh-sor-us) – a dinosaur which had very short legs and looked like a big crocodile, but had a beak like a snapping turtle instead of jaws full of teeth. The name rhynchosaurus means 'beaked lizard'.

Triassic (try-as-sick) – from about 200 to 250 million years ago, during this time period seed plants and spiney trees flourished on land along with many species of reptiles and, eventually, the first dinosaurs.

Look out!
We're racing out of the shadows ...

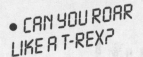